Kansas A to Z

A is for Airplane.

Airplanes made in Kansas
glide through the big blue sky.

B is for Buffalo.

Buffalo roam the prairie grazing on green grasses that turn red and brown.

C is for Cowboy.

Cowboys and cowgirls
rope cattle on big ranches.

D is for Depot.

Depots welcome people to ride big black trains.

E is for Eisenhower.

Eisenhower felt pride growing up in Kansas.
He grew to be 34th president of the
United States.

F is for Farmer.

Farmers drive tractors. They plow fields, plant seeds, and harvest food for us to eat.

G is for Grasshopper.

Grasshoppers hop through Kansas gardens
eating everything they see.

H is for "Home on the Range."

Home on the range is where the deer and the antelope play.

I is for Insect.

Insects buzz around Kansas.
The yellow and black honeybee
works hard to make sweet honey.

J is for Jackrabbit.

Jackrabbits zigzag through gardens. With their big brown ears they listen for visitors.

K is for Kansa.

Kansa Indians were some of the
first people to live in Kansas.
The state is named for them.

L is for Limestone.

Limestone dug out of the ground
can be used to build things.
Limestones fence farmers' fields.

M is for Meadowlark.

Meadowlarks sing little songs and make their nests of grasses.

N is for Nature.

Nature is all around us. Tall cottonwood trees drink cool water from rivers and streams.

O is for Oxen.

Oxen pulled covered wagons across the prairie to help pioneers find new homes.

P is for Prairie.

Prairie grasses, big and tall,
dance gracefully in the wind.

Q is for Quail.

Quail hide in farm fields
and tall grasses. They love
to run instead of fly.

R is for Roads.

Roads crisscross Kansas
packed with cars
and trucks.

S is for Snake.

Snakes slither onto rocks to warm in the sun.
They can be brown, red, or green.

T is for Train.

Trains chug across Kansas. There are old steam engines and shiny new diesels.

U is for Underground.

Underground is where
salamanders live. Shiny
and wet they slip out at night.

V is for Violet.

Violet skies are part of Kansas.
In the evening the sunset sparkles
with reds and blues painting violet skies.

W is for Wheat.

Wheat grows tall in Kansas producing flour to make bread and other good things to eat.

X is for X marks the spot.

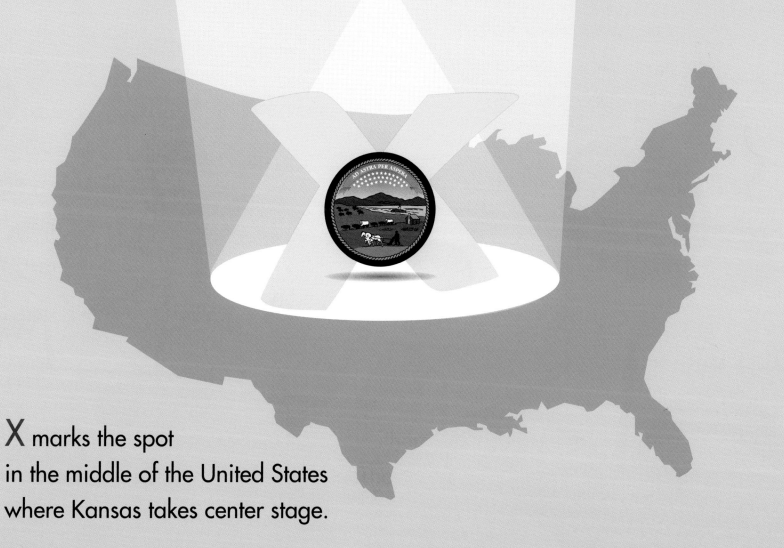

X marks the spot
in the middle of the United States
where Kansas takes center stage.

Y is for Yellow.

Yellow sunflowers grow strong. The flowers stretch and bend to the sun each day.

Z is for Zither.

Zithers make beautiful music.
The strings pluck out a lovely melody
for Kansas kids.

It's clear to see
from A to Z
Kansas is
the best place to be!